# *EMILY*
## *and the*
## *Santa Fe Trail*

**Evelyn A. Bartlow**

**Illustrated by Linda Newton**

ROCK CREEK PRESS
Shawnee Mission, Kansas

Acknowledgements: Sincere thanks to family and friends for help and encouragement.

Dedicated to the Santa Fe Trail and to those who have a love affair with it and all other old trails.

Published by
Rock Creek Press, L.L.C.
10167 Haskins Street
Shawnee Mission, KS 66215-1857

Library of Congress Catalog Card Number: 97-75944
ISBN: 1-890826-04-9

Printed in the United States of America
First Edition: January 1998

10 9 8 7 6 5 4 3 2

# PROLOGUE

EMILY JOHNSON'S STORY BEGINS EARLY ON THE MORNING of June 10, 1846. Emily is a fictitious character but she represents a type of girl who lived on the new frontier and wanted more from life than the restrictive Victorian beliefs of her day allowed for young women.

This story is based in part on Susan Shelby Magoffin's true account of a trip by covered wagon to Santa Fe. During the summer of 1846, Mrs. Magoffin recorded her impressions as she accompanied her husband Samuel, a veteran trader, on the long, arduous journey along the trail. Her travel diary, published many years later as *Down the Santa Fe Trail and into Mexico*, was one of the first journals written by a woman in nineteenth century America.

The historical setting of this story is real. From its founding in 1827 until 1856, Independence, Missouri, served as a main outfitting point for Santa Fe traders. Goods bought in St. Louis, New York, Philadelphia and even as far away as Europe were shipped up the Missouri River to this site where they were transferred at several landings from steamboats to freight wagons bound for Santa Fe.

As the story opens, twelve-year-old Emily has ridden in the freight wagon with her father, Matthew Johnson, a Santa Fe trader, and her brother Jed, ten, from the family farm near Independence to the Wayne City Landing on the Missouri River.

Matt Johnson works for Aull's Mercantile Company. Each spring for several years he has loaded a Conestoga wagon with cargo from the company and made the long trip west to sell the goods. He knows the wagon train will be a welcome sight to the 4,000 residents of Santa Fe who are isolated from good roads and navigable rivers. Dry goods, foodstuffs and hardware brought by traders help to give them a better life.

While Matt is occupied at the waterfront, Emily and Jed wait by their wagon for the roustabouts to unload their cargo.

*"Papa . . . please let me go with you."*

## CHAPTER 1

WHOA! WHOA!" A VOICE BOOMED, its echo resounding from the limestone bluffs along the Missouri River. As the voice came nearer, Emily saw a large bearded man yanking the reins to get control of a team of runaway mules hitched to a wagon. She turned and watched as the mules stumbled on uneven ground and the wagon lurched, scattering men and beasts to each side of the hill. That is, she watched until the mules and wagon headed straight in her direction and suddenly swerved toward her brother and their wagon.

"Jed—under the wagon! Quick!" Emily screamed, trying to make her small voice heard over the jangling harness and shouts of men.

Jed dived headlong between the wheels of their own wagon. Seconds later the runaway mules trampled over the very spot where he had stood.

Emily's feet strewed small pebbles as she hurried to the back of the wagon and waited for Jed to crawl from under the tailgate. "Come on out," she said. "It's safe now."

Matt Johnson ran up the slope from the waterfront just as his son rolled out from under the wagon, covered with dust and straw. Jed put his hand to his head where a trickle of blood was beginning to run down the side of his face. He sat down on the ground and leaned against the spokes of the wagon wheel, looking a little dazed.

"Oh, Jed, are you hurt? Papa—"

"Come here, son. How did you cut your head?"

"I must've hit it on the tar pot when I slid under the wagon,"

1

Jed answered. He stood up and almost lost his balance.

Matt steadied Jed with one hand and with the other wiped blood from his face with a bandana. "That's a bad cut." He frowned. "Maybe you should go back home and stay with Mama."

"I don't want to go home. I want to go with you. Please, Papa." Jed shoved his hand into the pocket of his trousers. "I still have the tally stick," he said, waving it high above his head.

"Well . . . we'll see. Let's keep loading. When we're finished I'll decide if you are able to go with me to Santa Fe or if you should go home." Matt motioned to the roustabouts to go back to work now that the runaway team had been reined in. "Bring the next load," he shouted.

A swarm of laborers rolled heavy barrels and carried cumbersome boxes down the gangway to the waiting wagon. Matt watched the loading of the cargo to make sure it wouldn't shift during the bumps and jolts on the long trip ahead.

Jed continued to keep track of each delivery by whittling notches on his wooden tally stick. When the loaders pulled two heavy bolts of white cotton cloth to the rear of the wagon, he cut two shallow notches in the stick. After a keg of nails was added, he made one deep cut in the wood.

A clash of noises from the waterfront bombarded Emily's ears—a loud blast from a steamboat whistle, shouts and curses of men, and the braying of mules. Early summer breezes blew loose hay, chicken feathers, and earthy odors into the air. She had to talk to Papa, and she had to do it soon before the wagon train pulled out. Her heart beat a little faster. She wanted to go! Ever since her eighth birthday she had helped Papa get ready for his trips to Santa Fe, and now she was twelve—almost grown up. But every time she asked to go along, he always said, "No, women and girls don't travel the trail."

She plopped down on a nearby wooden barrel and squirmed to get comfortable on the hard lid, determined to wait for the right moment. She yanked a faded sunbonnet down low on her head and tied the strings snugly under her chin to keep the wind from lifting it skyward. Her long brown braid with golden highlights hung all the way to her waist, and she could feel it swinging like a pendulum across her back as she turned her head this way and that to watch the men loading the wagon.

Each roustabout walked behind Emily on his return to the

steamship. She sensed that someone was near and turned around to see a young man who had stopped to admire and point at her swinging braid. Two other youths watched in amusement as he tried to make her blush by calling her "Blue Eyes."

Emily refused to smile and waved them away. "Go on. Go on." She knew they were only teasing, but she had more important things on her mind. She shook the dust from the folds of her faded blue calico dress and watched for Papa.

Matt approached the wagon with a piece of paper in his hand. He stopped beside her.

"Papa, oh, please may I go with you this time?" She tugged at her father's sleeve. "I'm two years older than Jed. I can shoot a gun. And cook. And walk a long way."

Matt ignored her and before she finished talking he had already turned to tell another trader he would like a ride to Independence to buy staples before they had to leave. "We'll load the saws and axes and then we'll be ready to go into town with you," he said. "Emily, you stay here and watch the wagon while we're gone."

He handed Jed a slip of paper, and Emily read over her brother's shoulder the quantities of food needed for the round trip to Santa Fe:

150 pounds of flour
150 pounds of bacon
30 pounds of coffee beans
60 pounds of sugar
5 pounds of salt

"Why can't I go on the trail with you?" Emily persisted. "I'm strong, and Jed's hurt . . . "

Again, Matt didn't seem to hear her. The rumble of the other trader's wagon drowned her plea. She would have to try another plan to persuade him. She promised herself she *would* find a way.

3

## CHAPTER 2

EMILY THOUGHT ABOUT ALL HER FAMILY HAD DONE to prepare for this trip. She knew that having adequate provisions was important to surviving the long journey to Santa Fe. Most of the food Papa was taking had been grown on the family farm. They had produced beans and corn which were dried and easy to transport without spoiling, as well as the salted bacon from hogs they had raised. He also took a bucket of sourdough starter for making pancakes and breads and a supply of fresh eggs to be packed in the flour barrels. She and Mama had dried apples and peaches to send along. Mama said fruits were a necessary part of their diet to prevent scurvy, a skin disease that caused blotchy skin and bleeding gums. They could not run the risk of getting sick so far from home.

Emily walked over to the wagon and ran her hand lightly along the rough wooden side. She tried to imagine what it would be like to walk beside the big freighter loaded with enough foodstuffs to last twelve weeks and hauling 3,000 pounds of trade goods besides. Her dream of traveling the trail had deepened with each passing year, and she knew she could do it, if only . . .

A thunderous noise startled her back to the present. She looked toward the rock ledge in time see another Conestoga round the bend on its way to pick up goods from a waiting steamship. She retied her limp bonnet strings and pulled the brim lower to shade her face.

The rattling of metal wagon chains and shouts of "Whoa!" announced the men's return from Independence. Matt and Jed would leave for Santa Fe as soon as the wagon was loaded and the oxen were hitched.

Emily stood at the end of the wagon, and when she looked up she saw the sky divided by arches—nine wooden bows curved over the wagon bed to support the white ducking cover. The last barrel of nails and bolt of broadcloth had been packed tightly into the seventeen-foot wagon, and all that remained to be loaded were the staples they had just bought. First Emily buried the eggs in the flour barrel, then she loaded everything into the food box at the back of the wagon. When she had finished, Papa slammed the tailgate shut and bolted it.

Mr. Aull, owner of the Mercantile Store and Matt's employer, beckoned for Matt to come over to the stockpen gate. Emily could not hear what they were saying, but she saw Mr. Aull hand her father a package about the size of a loaf of bread, wrapped in blue paper. Matt smiled and they shook hands.

Papa strode back toward the wagon. "Emily, come get this package. Mr. Aull has asked me to deliver it for him in Santa Fe. Put it in a safe spot where it will be out of the dust and rain."

Emily took the package as he turned to the task of unfolding the canvas that was to be stretched over the wagon top. She gently squeezed the package. What ever could it be? Balancing on tiptoe, she reached over the backboard and placed the blue package in a protected space behind the food box. Since the ends of the wagon were built higher than the middle, and everything was tightly wedged in, there was little chance that the large, wooden food box would shift and crush the small package. She found a scrap of canvas which she placed on top of it, just in case the rain slanted in.

She wasn't aware that a tall, rather scrawny boy standing near the stock pen had watched her place the package inside their wagon. He disappeared behind the wooden fence before she turned around.

Matt looked up to see the tall boy approaching with long steps. The boy ran his fingers nervously through an unruly lock of sun-bleached hair.

"Mr. Johnson, sir, Hawk's my name—Hawk Hammond. I was wondering if you could use an extra hand with the livestock and things."

Matt looked the boy in the eye. "Well, as a matter of fact—my son's a little under the weather here. What can you do?"

"I'm real good with livestock, and my pa—he cooks and I've helped him a lot. I know how—"

"Oh, I know who you are now, Cookie Hammond's boy! He's the best trail cook anywhere around."

"I'd sure like a job."

"Hawk, let me think about it. I'll let you know."

## CHAPTER 3

"JED, DO YOU FEEL LIKE HELPING ME?" Papa called.

"Yes, Papa, my head doesn't hurt any more," he said.

"Let me look at that cut . . ." He nodded. "Not as bad as I feared." Motioning, he said, "Let's cover the wagon top. Remember how we did it last year?"

They spread the first sheet to cover all the wooden bows. They added two more layers of canvas so the hood would shed rain and keep the bolts of fabric dry. While they worked to pull the canvas tautly across the bows, Emily held the mule team and watched. She kept the reins wrapped tightly around her hands so there would be no more runaways.

She recalled the conversation she'd had with Mama just the day before.

"Mama, please, please talk with Papa and persuade him to let me go with him tomorrow," she had pleaded.

"I know how much you want to go to Santa Fe," her mother had said. "You've begged to go since you were a little girl. And I would miss you terribly—but I'm not afraid for you to go. Papa knows the trail, and he and Jed would take good care of you."

"Then, please ask him, Mama."

"This year it would be all right for you to leave. Your grandparents are coming from Ohio to look for a farm, and they'll be here to help me with the work while your father's gone." She had a faraway look in her eyes, almost as if she were trying to convince herself that it would be all right. "But, Emily, you know Papa's the head of the house. It's hard to get a man to change his mind."

7

"It's worth trying. I can help Papa. I can cook."

"Maybe tomorrow your father will change his mind and let you go . . . Why don't you ask him at the last minute?"

"Oh, do you think—?"

"You can ask, but I really don't know." Her mother shook her head. "In case he has a change of heart, let's roll an extra dress, shawl, tin plate and cup in a blanket and pack it in the back of the wagon tonight. And maybe a clean apron."

"Oh, yes, and my diary, too!" Emily clasped her hands together. The next minute she ran to find her diary and returned with the little leather-bound volume in a drawstring pouch she had made for it. It was her favorite possession, sent to her last year for Christmas by her grandmother in Ohio. She was glad she had sewn the cloth pouch which would make it easier to take care of the diary and would keep her from losing the quill pen and ink bottle she used for writing.

Mama blinked back tears, but she hid her sadness with a smile. Emily was still her little girl even when she had grownup ideas. She took a clean handkerchief from her apron pocket and handed it to Emily. "Here, you might need this."

"Jed, we're done," Papa said. "It's almost time to go. That cut looks like it's going to heal. I believe you are well enough to make the trip. Let's leave our mule team in the stock pen and yoke the oxen."

At the stock pen Papa and Jed quickly located their twelve oxen, put the wooden neck yokes in place, and hitched them to the covered wagon in six pairs. The 850-mile journey would soon begin.

## CHAPTER 4

"IS THE WATER BARREL FULL?" Papa shouted.

"Filled to the brim," Jed answered.

"Is the tar pot hanging from the back axle?"

"Yup, and it's full of pine tar and grease."

"You'll need to give the hubs a coat of tar pretty often so the wheels will turn smoothly," Papa instructed. "Water and tar are important. It gets mighty dry on the prairie."

Emily paced back and forth as she waited to talk to Papa. She retied her limp bonnet strings. She knew she was running out of time, and if she couldn't get him to change his mind she would be left behind.

She stepped in front of Papa as he headed for the front of the wagon.

"Papa, I have to talk to you."

"Hurry up and say what you have to say. We're ready to leave."

"I've tried all morning—but you haven't answered me. May I go to Santa Fe with you? Please let me go."

"Sunshine, you know women and girls don't travel the trail."

Emily's heart sank when he used the pet name he had called her as a little girl and repeated the old argument.

"But, Papa, I'm not a child! I can help you!"

"You would have to walk every step of the way because the wagon is packed full with trading goods."

"I'm a good walker. I know I can walk fifteen miles a day."

"You'll have to sleep on the ground. We'll have to deal with rain, hot weather, wind and dust. Each day the scouts will look for water and often it's hard to find. You will get thirsty. Cornmeal mush and salt pork won't taste like Mama's hot

9

biscuits and gravy that you love so much."

"You're telling me all the bad things. I've heard good things about the trail. I'd want to see the wildflowers we don't have in Missouri. I want to see the animals and birds you told us about, that live in the tall grasses. Besides, I can help you and Jed. I can gather fuel and cook for us."

Papa scratched his chin as he listened. Emily rushed on, her words tumbling out. "Yesterday in Aull's Mercantile Store a pretty lady told Mrs. Aull that she was going on the trail with her husband. She even asked if I was going. Oh, please—"

Emily watched him crisscross the rope across the tailgate. She saw crinkles appear around his eyes above the mustache that hid his smile. He winked and said, "Emily, how would you like to go to Santa Fe with Jed and me?"

"Oh, Papa, thank you!" She fairly danced with joy. She hopped on one foot and then the other. In her excitement she blurted out, "I have extra clothes in the wagon."

Papa pointed his finger at her. "I know. Your mother talked to me when I found your truck last night."

Emily grinned. "Oh, Papa . . ."

Matt made a mental note to tell the Hammond boy he wouldn't be needing him. He would also ask Mr. Aull to stop by the farm and tell Mama he had decided to take Emily to Santa Fe after all.

# CHAPTER 5

THE ROADS OF INDEPENDENCE, MISSOURI, bustled with activity as forty-five covered wagons were lined up to begin the long trek to Santa Fe.

"Yoke up! Yoke up!" the wagonmaster, Jake Summers, bellowed. The wagonmaster was aptly named for he was indeed the master of their wagons—captain of all the prairie schooners. Emily thought he was one of the tallest, most impressive men she had ever seen, except for Papa, of course.

The teams of oxen were prodded and shoved to the waiting freight wagons. Each trader hurried, trying to be the first to call out, "All's set."

"Catch up!" shouted the wagonmaster. Emily knew this order meant the men had to get the wagons rolling and into two lines.

Dust and noises filled the town square. Dogs barked and mules brayed. Whips cracked, wagon wheels creaked, and the swinging yoke chains clanged as the oxen lunged forward, straining to get their heavy loads rolling. Slowly the wagon wheels began to turn. Finally they were on their way to Santa Fe!

People waved from porches and windows as the caravan crept past the courthouse toward the edge of town. Emily smiled and waved back at children running alongside the moving wagons. She had spent most of her twelve years on the family farm north of Independence and never had a chance to see what lay beyond. Now she would finally get to see what she had only heard of through her father's stories.

Soon the wagons left behind the storefronts and houses and fell into a steady rhythm of rolling across mile after mile. They traveled through timbered creek bottoms and over green meadows ablaze with wildflowers. On each side of the trail grew familiar flowers—pale pink wild roses and blue lupines on one side and, on the other, lavender verbena and white shooting stars. In a sunny meadow were Indian paintbrush and black-eyed Susans. She would press her favorite flowers in the back of her diary for Mama.

Emily looked up from picking a sunflower to pin on her bonnet and saw two trail scouts on horseback ride up to Papa. It was their job to ride ahead each day to check the condition of the trail. She heard them tell Papa they had found level ground along a shallow stretch of the river where the wagons could cross safely.

At the crossing, the river flowed gently over a sandy bed. The plodding oxen pulled their heavily-loaded wagon through the water without incident. Papa walked alongside his team. As they started up the hill, he shouted "Gee" and cracked his whip over the head of the lead team. They had strayed too far to the right. Upon reaching the top of the swale, Papa shouted "Haw" and snapped the whip again. This time they had strayed too far left. The lead oxen, trained to respond to the driver's commands, guided the other teams into a straight line as soon as the trail stretched out along level ground.

By late morning a slight breeze had sprung up, but not enough to clear away the dust. When the sun was overhead, the travelers made a short stop to eat.

That afternoon Emily and Jed walked beside the wagon, trying to stay mostly in the shade cast by the wagon top.

"I'm glad our freighter is near the front of the train," Jed said. He looked back at the clouds of dust they were leaving. "But I wish I could see how many wagons are behind us."

"I haven't seen many people today—besides the drivers. Have you seen any women?" she asked.

Jed shook his head. "Tomorrow let's walk to the end of the wagon train and see the rest of the people who are going to Santa Fe."

Walls of tall prairie grass lined each side of the dusty road. Emily wanted to explore the narrow paths that branched off, but she knew she had better stay close to the wagon. She wondered if other girls lived at the ends of those trails. If so, what kinds of houses did they live in? She knew many of the paths were probably made by animals, hunting for food. She hoped she would see baby animals on the trip.

At sunset the weary travelers approached Barn's camping grounds where there were water and pasture for the oxen. Most of the day had been spent breaking in the new steers. The seasoned oxen helped the teamsters get the new animals used to the yoke and pulling in unison. Papa said it was a good day even though they had traveled only ten miles.

Emily walked proudly beside their majestic wagon as it rolled into the campground. Her hair and dress were covered with dust, and she was barefoot because her leather high-topped shoes had made her feet too warm. She almost had to pinch herself to believe it wasn't a dream. She really *was* traveling the Santa Fe Trail. It was incredible, but for the time being she was ready for a drink of cool water and something to eat.

Firewood couldn't be found around Barn's camp to cook an evening meal, so the Johnsons ate dried apples and hardtack [a hard cracker made with flour and water, no yeast]. Papa said fuel would be scarce as they traveled farther west. He pointed out the canvas hammock under the wagon and told them it was for storing any wood and dried bison chips they found along the way. Emily wrinkled her nose at the thought of having to pick up animal dung.

Emily and Jed located their blankets at the back of the wagon and unrolled them near the dying embers of the only campfire the caravan burned that night. Papa stopped to tell them he would be away for a while to stand nightwatch with the other traders.

"Be ready to leave early in the morning when the night herders wake us," he reminded them.

Jed soon fell asleep. Emily lit the candle lantern and reached for her diary. She pulled the pouch drawstrings apart, took out the quill pen, ink bottle and leather-bound diary. In the dim candlelight she began to write.

*In the dim candlelight she began to write.*

*Dear Diary,*

*Tonight is my first night away from home. I wonder what Mama is doing. I pressed some Queen Anne's lace for her.*

*I'm so glad Papa let me come. I'll show him how grown up I can be. I'll try to make the trip easier for him. I've already started to care for the blue package. I wonder what's in it. It's very light & soft when I squeeze it.*

*I felt like a little ant walking beside our giant wagon. I saw the animal trails that go back into the tall grass. My feet too are helping make a trail. Like the people & animals that traveled before me, I am a part of the Santa Fe Trail.*

*At sunset the sun changed into an orange ball that slid into the prairie grass. The clouds were edged in gold.*

*Jed & I are sleeping under the stars tonight.*

*Emily Johnson*

Emily lay on her blanket not far from the campfire ring. As darkness closed in on the circle of freighters, she watched the flickering flames create ghost-like shadows that danced on the canvas covers of the silent wagons.

The cool night air wrapped around the spokes of the wagon wheels. She shivered and pulled the flannel cover tightly around her shoulders. She closed her eyes and said her prayers. Then, lulled by the sounds of men snoring, oxen lowing and the winds rustling the prairies grasses, she drifted off to sleep.

During the night, some of the oxen, frightened by howling coyotes, tried to break out of the wagon circle. Sentries calmed them and anxiously waited for dawn to streak the eastern sky signaling an end to their long night of patrolling the camp.

CHAPTER 6

AT THE FIRST RAYS OF LIGHT, BIRDS BEGAN TO TWITTER. The night watchmen hurried  from wagon to wagon shouting "Arise"  and raking wooden tally sticks across the spokes of the wagon wheels. When the grating "bur-r-r-rum" sounded across their wagon wheels, Emily sat up, straight as a tally stick herself.

Emily looked over at Jed. "Wake up, sleepyhead. Time to get up." She quickly shook out her blanket. "Someone must have chickens. I can hear roosters crowing. Listen—I hear a meadowlark! It's singing 'It's spring of the year.' "

"I don't hear anything," Jed grumbled, covering his head.

Emily rolled her blanket into a ball and tucked it just inside the tailgate. In a few minutes her sleepy brother had put on his shoes and also was ready to go.

Waiting teamsters listened for the call to get going. The wagonmaster shouted "Catch Up!"  Drivers hurried past Emily to hitch their teams.  She heard the familiar calls,  "Hep, hep," "Get along there!"  and "Giddy-up."  The teamsters lined up, eager to be on the trail.  Soon the caravan was on its way. Ho! to  Santa Fe.

The wagon train rumbled along in the cool morning hours. Since no wood was available for cooking, previous campers having burned it all, Papa, Jed and Emily satisfied their hunger by eating hardtack  and dried apples as they walked along. Earlier that morning the scouts had ridden ahead and found a grassy pasture near Brush Creek where they could stop long enough to rest the animals and prepare a midday meal.

Jed and Emily searched for fuel as they moved along the trail

16

and tossed the few scraps of wood they found into the hammock under the wagon. Emily bent down and reached in the grass for a half-hidden piece of firewood. The small log was snatched out of her hands by a youth who was taller than she. He turned and galloped off in the opposite direction, long legs flying.

She gathered up her skirt and ran after him. "That's mine! Give it back," she shouted. "Go find your own wood!"

Emily, as fleet-footed as most boys her age, caught him and grabbed one end of the big stick. A tug-of-war ensued until the wagonmaster walked toward them.

"That's a good piece to store in your hammock, Emily," he said.

The boy let go, and the incident was settled.

Emily had won the firewood but Papa, who had seen the whole skirmish, was not pleased. "It's not ladylike to lift your skirt above your knees and fight like boys do," he scolded. "That was the Hammond boy—Hawk, they call him—who offered to help me. I've a good notion to have you apologize . . ."

Around noon the caravan arrived at the creek. No trees grew on the banks, only small scrub brush, but water and grass were plentiful.

While Matt and Jed unhitched the oxen and led them to pasture to graze with the other animals, Emily busied herself with cooking her first meal. She built a small fire and looked for her cooking utensils. Everything was different from Mama's kitchen and there was no place to set anything. She stirred the cornmeal mush to keep it from sticking. The salt pork had to be sliced, when she could locate a knife, and she must not forget to make Papa's coffee. For a special treat she made a big skillet of scrambled eggs. Finally everything was done at once, and she set out the tin plates on a cloth. She put a sunflower in the middle, remembering that Mama often put flowers on the table to please Papa.

During their meal Papa told the children about the small covered wagons that had just passed their caravan. He said they were on their way to Oregon. The wagons carried whole families who sometimes packed up their furniture and left behind relatives and friends they would never see again. Going to Oregon was a much harder trip than the one to Santa Fe. It would take them nearly six months to travel the 2,000 miles.

Emily had one question: "Why? Why do they go?"

Papa was quiet for a moment. "They're pioneers," he said. "They hope to find a better life than the one they left."

He told them to watch for a weatherbeaten sign that read "ROAD TO OREGON" at the next fork in the trail. That was where the Oregon Trail diverged to the northwest, while the Santa Fe Trail continued westward.

Emily scrubbed the Dutch oven with sand, cleaned the other utensils and stored them in the wagon. She was relieved to see Papa in a better mood.

In the middle of the afternoon the wagonmaster called, "Stre-etch out!" The hitching up process was repeated, and the long caravan was on the trail again.

That night they traveled late. A bright moon lit the trail, and they made good time in the cool evening. Emily liked traveling at night when the moon cast a white glow over the landscape.

Step by step, mile by mile, one exciting discovery after another, Emily experienced the daily routine along the trail. For a week the caravan continued to travel across the open plain toward Council Grove. The level land made it an easy trip for drivers and animals.

During one of their rest stops, Emily got her chance to examine more closely the other freight wagons and various travelers that made up the motley procession.

"Jed, let's walk to the back of the wagon train." She counted the white hoods as they walked between the two lines of freighters. "Most of the wagons are Conestogas like ours. Look at that little black carriage. Does it have trading goods in it? It looks so small."

"I don't think it carries anything to sell in Santa Fe," Jed answered. "Last year there was another little wagon like that. Papa said it was owned by somebody who wanted to ride all the way."

"I wouldn't want to ride in a little black box all the way. I'd rather walk some of the time." Emily said in a loud whisper, "Let's get closer and see what's in it." They walked around to the side. "Aww . . . " she said, "All the windows are covered. All I can see is—"

"*Ninguno! Ninguno!*" [No! No!] the young Mexican driver said in a low voice. He put a hand across his mouth as if making a sign for them to be quiet.

"We're just looking at this part of the wagon train," Emily explained timidly.

The driver shook his finger and motioned them away.

"We aren't hurting anything. We only wanted to see who was in your little wagon," Jed said.

"*Irse marcharse!*" [Go away!] the driver persisted, scowling and shaking his head.

"I don't think he understands. Jed, let's get out of here before he really gets mad."

They turned around and headed back toward their own wagon. Jed pulled out his red bandana and wiped his face.

"Why is his part of the wagon train so special that we can't go back there?" Emily complained. She lifted her skirt so that she could walk faster.

They reached their wagon as a trail scout approached on horseback. "Council Grove is just ahead," he told Papa. "There's plenty of hardwood, water and grass there! We can rest for a few days before we head on down the trail. The wagonmaster says to be sure to make any repairs you need and get replacement parts for your wagon because we won't find much hardwood west of Council Grove."

*Day 10*

*Dear Diary,*

*Papa was cranky with me this morning. It was so warm under my blanket, I didn't want to get up. I couldn't tell if I should wear my shoes today or walk without them.*

*My chores on the trail are different from the things I do at home. I'm trying to cook good meals. I want Papa to be glad he brought me.*

*The grasses are full of animals & birds. Jed & I followed two little 'possums that waddled off into their hideout. We found a nest of baby rabbits. Swarms of grasshoppers fly in our faces, & we have to brush them out of our hair & clothes. The sky turns white when the sun catches their wings. They strike the ground like hail & the wagon wheels grind them into dust.*

*Tomorrow—a place where trees grow.*

*Before I blow my candle out, I'll check the blue package.*

*E. J.*

19

# CHAPTER 7

A N UPROAR OF JOYOUS WHOOPING AND SHOUTING broke out. Papa, who was usually serious, threw his hat in the air and caught it. "There's Council Grove!" he shouted. It was their first important milestone.

The wagons stopped along a high ridge overlooking a rushing river that flowed between tree-lined banks. After many days of traveling the rolling prairie with its sun-dried grasses and only a few spindly cottonwoods, the men welcomed the sight of the lush green trees. The settlement had become a meeting place for travelers all around, especially those looking to join a caravan.

Emily never imagined she would be so glad to see water— lots of it—and trees—oak, hickory, elm and walnut. She clasped her hands together and skipped over beside Papa to get a better view.

"Why do they call it 'Council Grove'?" she asked.

"The Osage Indians and some white men met and signed a treaty there by that big grove of trees," he said, pointing. "It's a natural stopping place for travelers and now, in exchange for money and goods, the tribe lets American and Spanish caravans pass through their land. Some other Indian tribes, whose land we'll soon be passing through, haven't signed treaties with us." He looked at his only daughter, so unaware of the real dangers in this untamed land, and smoothed the unruly fringes of hair away from her eyes. "I hope we won't have trouble farther on," he said.

Emily followed the wagons down into Council Grove where she got a closer look at the sparkling Neosho River. Papa joined the other traders as they led their oxen into a grassy pasture.

Papa told Jed and Emily there was an oak tree up by the tent store that was used as a post office. They decided to write a letter to Mama and leave it in the knothole in the tree fork in hopes that someone traveling to Independence would deliver it.

Later Papa returned from a meeting held to elect a new captain for the caravan. Jake Summers, who had served as wagonmaster since they left Independence, had been chosen for his vast experience on the trail and his knowledge of military organization.

Captain Summers began immediately to organize for the rest of the trip. He divided the forty-five Conestoga wagons into four groups and appointed Matt as one of his four lieutenants. To simplify their mealtime routines, he also formed them into "messes" with ten people in each one.

"We need a cook for our mess," Papa said, "and, Emily, I want you to be our cook. Can you do that?"

"Oh, Papa, I know I can," Emily said.

"Your only duty, when you're in camp, is to cook the meals. The others in our mess will carry water, gather fuel for the campfire, clean up and stand guard. Do you think you can cook for that many men, Sunshine?"

"I'll be glad to! I'll do my best to cook good meals for our mess."

"Or make a mess of the meals," Jed offered.

Matt made arrangements to borrow a cook wagon in Council Grove and leave it off on the way back. Then he assigned one of the men, Shorty, to drive it. Emily took stock of their supplies and shopped at the tent store for sowbelly, beans and other foods for the trip. The ten people in their group brought over all their foodstuffs and utensils, and she sorted and placed them in the cook wagon.

When she had finished, Emily brushed the stray hairs away from her face and straightened her shoulders. She felt proud that her father trusted her with such an important job.

Later the teamsters gathered around Emily to offer their congratulations and suggestions.

"Ma'am, I'll have cherry pie with cream for dessert tomorrow night," Shorty said, his straw hat in his hand and his hair sticking up in all directions.

"How about a pot roast with carrots, onions, potatoes and gravy?" requested another driver they called "T. J."

"How about salt pork, cornmeal mush, dried apples and

21

coffee?" Emily retorted. "I'll do the best I can with what I have to work with until you bring me something different to cook." She really did not mind their comments when they smiled and were so willing to help to her.

Nearby, Hawk overheard the teamsters teasing Emily. "This trip is for men only!" he said to his brother. "Why did she have to tag along? I asked her father for a job, but he gave it to her—to a girl."

His brother was intent on carving a whistle from a willow branch and did not look up.

Thirteen-year old Hawk turned his back and walked away. "I'll bet I could make her sorry she came," he muttered.

"How much longer will we stay in Council Grove?" Emily asked her father the next day.

"We'll leave early tomorrow morning. The oxen are rested, the wagons repaired, and we're almost ready to go. Now let's get a good night's sleep."

*Day 12*

*Dear Diary,*

*I can't believe there is a place like Council Grove in the middle of the desert! There are lots of traders here & hundreds of cattle & mules.*

*Down at the river I washed our clothes with the lye soap Mama & I made. It feels so good to have enough water to bathe in.*

*I wrote to Mama about how I am helping Papa by being his cook. She will be pleased because she started teaching me to cook when I was five years old.*

*I've packed the blue package between some cloth bolts to keep it away from the dust.*

*I still wonder who's in that little black carriage & why they keep to themselves.*

*Jed & I watched the prairie dogs play. They visit from hole to hole. They are frisky & bark at each other. If we come too close, they go underground. He told me not to lay my blanket over their holes because they have fleas!*

*I'll try to please Papa with my cooking.*

*E. J.*

## CHAPTER 8

A T DAYBREAK, EMILY AND THE SLEEPING TRADERS were awakened by the night guards. Black clouds rolling across the western sky were streaked by intermittent flashes of lightning. The men hurried to bring water and build a fire for Emily to cook breakfast before the rain began. She quickly filled the pots with water and set them to boil. While the mush bubbled and the sowbelly fried, she lifted the lid of the coffee pot and out slithered a big grass snake!

"Oh!" Emily put her hand over her mouth because she didn't want the men to know she had a problem on her first day to cook for them. She shooed the snake away, washed the coffee pot, and put the coffee on the fire to simmer, as if nothing had happened. She was sure she had put the lid on tight when she put it away, but maybe not . . .

The men ate their big bowls of mush, with crumbled salt pork in it, and drank lots of coffee. She had wanted to bake cornbread and have enough left for the midday meal, but there was not enough time to let the fire burn down to coals for baking. It was already starting to sprinkle. As the claps of thunder grew louder she rushed to store the pots and pans in the cook wagon.

Turbulent winds whipped the tall prairie grasses around them like ocean waves. Emily tied her bonnet strings in a double knot and wrapped her wool plaid shawl around her shoulders. Handlers scurried to control the livestock. Most of the animals huddled together with their backs to the wind. The storm brought sheets of rain that whipped bits of grass and sand through camp. She and some of the men dived under the freight wagons to avoid the downpour. Hailstones struck the canvas

. . . out slithered a big grass snake!

wagon tops and balls of ice quickly covered the ground. In a few minutes the sudden storm was over, leaving everyone drenched.

After the hail melted, the trail, which had been deep with dust, became a muddy mire. Gushing waters had cut a channel between the trees that grew along Cottonwood Creek. Its banks were not steep, but the rain-soaked soil made them slippery. Most of the oxen managed to pull the wagons across the creek and up the slick bank. But one ox lost its footing and fell, causing the wagon to slide sideways into the stream. It was beyond the power of the other yoked oxen to move the wagon.

Matt waded over to the downed ox. "You're all right," he said as he gently stroked its shoulder. He braced a wooden pole under the animal as a lever to steady and help lift its weight. Then he prodded it with the toe of his shoe, urging it to get up. The frightened animal struggled to its feet. Together the teamsters and oxen pushed and pulled the wagon out of the mud, onto firmer ground.

While the men struggled with the wagon, Emily walked along the creek bank. She picked up colorful pebbles in places where the rain had washed the soil away. She heard rustling in the tall grasses and weeds that sounded like an animal rummaging around. The noise stopped. She listened, then continued looking for rocks. The grasses rustled again. She peered around a tall clump of weeds and came face to face with the pretty lady she had seen in Aull's store the day before they left Independence.

Both the lady and Emily were startled, but relieved to see each other instead of a wild animal. Each held a handful of pebbles.

Emily laughed. "You like to hunt small rocks too?" she asked.

The lady didn't speak but daintily lifted her skirt to step across a mud puddle, moving closer.

"My name's Emily, what's yours?"

"I'm Susan Magoffin," she answered.

"My father's a trader and I'm going to Santa Fe with him and my brother. Who are you with?"

"I'm traveling with my husband Samuel who is also a Santa Fe trader," Susan answered. They chatted for awhile and showed each other the pretty rocks they had found. They discovered it was the first trip for both of them, and they both were keeping an account of the trip in a diary.

Emily thought Susan was pretty with her smooth, creamy skin and her shiny black hair pulled back and tucked into a roll at the nape of her neck. She wore a necklace that was a small gold heart on a chain. In her light blue dress, she looked as if she were going to a party instead of traveling the Santa Fe Trail.

"Samuel and I have been married just eight months," she confessed, "so this is a big adventure for both of us. When we get to Pawnee Rock we are going to climb up on it and carve our names." Susan's blue eyes danced when she smiled, and she smiled a lot.

"Papa says there are hundreds of names on it." Emily felt comfortable talking to the young woman who even as an adult still seemed to have a childlike sense of wonder. "I wish I could climb that big rock—"

"Catch up," Captain Summers' voice interrupted.

"We'd better get back to our wagons," Susan said. "I'll see you along the way."

After the rainstorm the captain  began to reestablish order along the caravan.  He sent the trail scouts ahead to find a good camp site where the tired travelers could rest.

Before long Emily heard gunshots, snapping bullwhips and the whinny of frightened horses. "Papa, what are they shooting?"

"There are rattlesnakes ahead. The rain has flushed them out," Papa said. "We can't take the chance that they might bite our people or animals, so the men are riding ahead to clear the area of snakes. Better watch where you walk."

The captain had a quick word with Matt. "It's going to take the trail scouts longer than I thought. While we are waiting, could you have your children walk back along the trail and check for stray oxen?"

Matt nodded and sent Jed and Emily on their way. She took a stick with her,  both as a prod for the oxen and for protection from the snakes.

They walked  past where the long line of damp, white-topped Conestoga wagons had traveled and followed the muddy ruts into the tall prairie grass to look for strays.

"Look in the valley.  See those two oxen eating grass?"

26

"Where?" Jed asked. "Now I see them. Papa said if we find any strays, we are to be careful not to startle them and to try to herd them back."

Emily squinted her eyes. She saw in the distance a small band of men on horseback riding over the hills, their red waist sashes fanning out behind them. As the riders came closer she saw that they had heavy rifles strapped to their saddles. She had overheard Papa and the captain talking about the desperadoes from Mexico who stole and plundered lone wagons.

"Jed, they're riding toward the two oxen. I hope they won't steal them."

Jed and Emily hid in the tall grass and watched. They were almost afraid to breathe, the armed men rode by so close. And then a strange thing happened.

"Emily, I can't believe it. They rode right up to the oxen, shook their heads and waved their arms around and left. I wonder why?" Then they noticed their own trail scouts riding nearby.

Emily and Jed ran all the way back to the wagons.

"We found two stray oxen," Jed told Captain Summers, trying to catch his breath. "We saw men with guns looking them over, but the men went away. They looked like outlaws, but they didn't steal the strays. Something must have spooked them. But I'll bet they have a camp not far from here."

"Thanks for warning us, Jed," the captain said. "We will assign more men to patrol the caravan. The trail scouts are back and I will send them to herd the strays in with the other cattle."

Twelve days later the caravan had covered many more miles of the trail. At sundown a thunderstorm came up, and the freighters stopped in the road to wait for it to end. First there was a warning of forked lightning followed by growling thunder. Then strong winds and a drenching rain battered the travelers.

After the storm subsided, darkness soon fell. But they continued to move on. A pale light from the moon appeared from under murky clouds between lightning flashes. The wagons traveled until midnight and finally stopped near a high mound of sandstone—Pawnee Rock. The caravan made its usual corral by forming a circle with wagons, running them as close behind each other as possible with the left-hand side innermost.

"Papa, Jed and I want to climb Pawnee Rock and cut our names in it—" Emily began.

"No, it's too dangerous. The moonlight isn't bright enough for you to see, and the sandstone could be slippery from the rain. I can't go with you, because I'm on guard duty tonight. Maybe you can carve your names there on our way back. We'll see. Now roll your blankets out under the wagon and get to sleep."

Papa's words left no room for argument.

*Day 24*

*Dear Diary,*

*When I told Papa about the snake in the coffee pot he got real mad at me & said I was careless when I put the coffee pot away. He hurt my feelings. Tonight I packed my pots & pans so snakes & other creatures can't get into them.*

*I miss Mama. I wish I could see her. Should I have come?*

*I was glad to meet the pretty lady again after the rainstorm. We like many of the same things. I hope to see her again.*

*The wind makes it hard to cook the meals & walk the trail. I am getting tanned. Mama wouldn't approve. With all the men around I don't have any privacy. I even have to hide behind the wagon to brush & braid my hair.*

*The ants are a problem in the sandy soil. I shake the bedding to be sure no ants are hiding in the folds. I've wrapped the blue package with an extra piece of canvas to keep the ants out.*

*This has been a long day. I'm tired & feeling sorry for myself. But rain or shine, fleas or ants, I still like traveling the trail.*

*E. J.*

# CHAPTER 9

O N THE HORIZON A CLOUD OF DUST ROLLED toward the wagon train. As the dust settled a mounted band of soldiers appeared. They carried an American flag and, as they drew closer, it was easy to distinguish their leader, dressed in a smart blue uniform.

He approached the trail boss, Captain Summers. "There's trouble on the trail," he said. "Your caravan can't travel on to Santa Fe until soldiers from Fort Leavenworth arrive to escort you through Indian territory. Your orders are to continue on to Bent's Fort and wait there until the escort arrives. If you take the trail along the Arkansas River, it'll take several weeks to reach Bent's Fort. You must stay there for your own protection."

"We haven't had any trouble  so far, coming through the Osage Indian lands," the wagon train captain said.

"There are some hostile tribes between Pawnee Rock and Santa Fe that don't want wagons traveling through their tribal grounds and destroying the bison," the commander told him. "They'll try to stop you!  That's why the government has issued an order to the cavalry to detain all wagons. You're to wait at Bent's Fort until troops can escort you on to Santa Fe."

Emily listened to the conversation between the two leaders with a tight feeling in the pit of her stomach. Shivers of fear ran up her back.

Weeks later, Captain Summers prepared the wagon train to set up camp at Bent's Fort while waiting for a military escort. He had located a meadow, just outside the fort, large enough to form a square enclosure. The ten wagons in Matt's  group were first to arrive and start the security formation. In the middle of the afternoon, the second and third groups of wagons joined them and formed two more sides. Toward sunset, the fourth group of freighters arrived in their fourteen Conestogas and completed the square.

Emily and Jed heard a loud "Whoa!" and saw the black Rockaway carriage stop at the main entrance of Bent's Fort, a big iron gate. The driver yelled again at the mule team, jumped to the ground and seemed to be having difficulty forcing the carriage door open. The black paint on one side was covered with dried mud. A dark-haired man stepped out of the door first and extended his hand back to someone in the wagon. It was Susan! He helped her out as if helping an invalid. As soon as the young woman had eased down the steps, a little brown dog with a long tail jumped out and followed her closely. A guard opened the gate, and Susan walked slowly into the fort with the man holding one arm and a woman holding the other.

Emily watched the scene with dismay. "She could walk without help when we hunted for pretty rocks," she told her brother.

That night Emily prepared her usual meal of salt pork, dried apples and coffee, but she also baked a Dutch oven full of golden cornbread. While they camped near Bent's Fort she would continue to prepare the same fare from her supplies in the cook wagon. No one complained, but she longed for fresh meat or an oven so that she could cook a real feast for Papa and Jed and the hungry men.

After the meal, Papa joined Shorty, T. J. and the other men around the campfire, where they drank more coffee and told outrageous trail stories. While she washed her cooking utensils, she listened to boasts about the number of grizzly bears they had killed from Missouri to Santa Fe. T. J. told stories about medicine men and their magic. Still another trader's tale was about old Davey Brown who was captured by the Indians. It seemed he let out a yell and jerked off his wig. He lived to tell the story and became known as "White-Man-Who-Scalps-Himself!"

As soon as she was finished with the clean-up, Emily asked Papa's permission to go inside the fort to see if she could find Susan. She had only seen the inaccessible walls of the big fort from the outside and, besides wanting to locate her friend, she was curious about what might be inside. Papa told her the fort was built of mud bricks, or adobe, because only a few trees grew in the area. The Bents had used Mexican workers and oxen to trample the straw, sand and water into mud. Then they had packed the mud mixture into wooden molds and placed them in the sun to dry. Cottonwood logs were hauled in to provide a framework for the hard, sun-baked bricks that were stacked together with mud to build the high, thick walls around the fort. After Papa's lecture on the structure of the fort, he told Emily she could go inside if she wouldn't stay too long.

At the main gate, Emily convinced the guard she had a good reason for wanting to go inside. What an array of people and activities greeted her eyes as she entered! She walked into a large courtyard, one hundred feet on every side, lined by rooms all around the walls. The fort was crowded to overflowing. Other travelers also had been halted by the army, and traders had come in for wagon repairs. The Cheyennes and Arapahos had brought pelts to trade for beads, tobacco, knives and utensils from the one small store inside the fort. Traders, craftsmen, and people of every description mingled in the big open courtyard.

Emily heard different languages being spoken by those she passed. She recognized the sounds of English, Spanish and French similar to the languages she heard each spring in Independence during the wagon train departures. She was puzzled by the sign language and gutteral words of the Native Americans.

She heard the sounds of a carpenter sharpening an ax on a grinding wheel and the clanging of a blacksmith's hammer shaping metal on an anvil. She was curious about an arch-shaped wooden form located in the center of the courtyard. An older man saw her interest, stopped his work of sprinkling water on the dirt floor, and said, "That wood frame is a fur press. It can squeeze 80 pounds of hides into a small bale which makes them easier to load and ship on wagons."

Emily wandered around the ground level of the two-story adobe compound looking for Susan's room. Some were sleeping rooms for those who lived there; others were used to carry on the work of the fort, but all had dirt floors. Finally she saw the man who had helped Susan out of the wagon, and the little brown dog was lying at his feet.

"Is Susan Magoffin in this room?" Emily asked.

"Yes, and I'm her husband Samuel. You must be Emily. She told me about you," he said. "She isn't feeling well."

"I'm sorry," Emily said. "What happened to her?"

"We were at Ash Creek where the bank was a little steep. We

31

decided to get out of the carriage and walk down. I yelled several times to the driver to stop and let us out, but he didn't hear me," Samuel said. "At the top of the hill, the wheel hit a rut and the wagon overturned. Susan was hurt. She needs to rest, but you can go in to see her for a few minutes."

Emily tiptoed into the dark room. Susan sat propped against pillows in a bed.

"Hello, I'm sorry you were hurt," Emily said softly. "Can I do anything for you?"

Susan moved slightly in the bed. Her face was pale and dark circles emphasized her large eyes. "No, but thank you anyway. A doctor who lives at the fort has been taking care of me. My husband Samuel and my maid Jane are also helping." Her usual smile was a little weak.

Emily shifted her weight from one foot to the other.

Susan brightened. "I do have something you could help with. Would you walk Bruno, my dog, while we are here? He needs the exercise."

"Yes, I'll be glad to walk him as often as you want," she answered eagerly. She noticed, even in the dark room, how the light reflected from the gold necklace Susan still wore. "I'd better go now. I'll come back and see you tomorrow. I saw your husband in the courtyard and I can ask him about walking your dog."

"Thank you, Emily," Susan said softly.

Guards began herding those who did not live in the fort toward the big iron gate. Emily thanked the man who had admitted her and hurried to get through the gate before it was locked for the night.

That night Emily was anxious to tell Jed all about the things she had seen inside the fort. "Bent's Fort is the biggest place I've ever seen," she began. "I thought our courthouse in Independence was large, but it would fit into one corner of the fort." She waited for Jed to answer, but she heard only the sound of his even breathing.

"Good night, Jed." She crawled into her blanket. She was too tired to light her lantern and write in her diary. Before she fell asleep she looked into the sky and wondered if the stars were brighter in this part of the country, or was it her imagination?

32

# CHAPTER 10

THE SUN ROSE WITH AN EARLY MORNING GLOW that burnished the mountains rising far to the west. The fort was already crowded with people, inside and out. As Emily passed through the gate she saw Cheyenne women and children on the outside gathered in a huddle, waiting for their men to finish trading their furs. Three Arapaho braves carrying pelts paid no attention to her as they entered the fort at the same time.

Emily walked as quickly as she could through the bustling courtyard until she reached Susan's room. Bruno heard her footsteps and began barking.

Susan was sitting up in bed with her diary on her lap. Jane had combed her hair and she wore a pretty pink bed jacket.

"I'll take Bruno for a walk down by the creek," she told Susan, "and when I get back, would you feel like talking to me?"

"Of course, dear. I'll look for you later on," Susan said.

The little dog sniffed and hunted around clumps of grass and fallen limbs, but no jackrabbits were to be found. He pulled Emily this way and that as he tugged energetically on his leash. In spite of their zig-zag course, she managed to pick a bouquet of wildflowers to take back to Susan.

A gentle wind rippled the grasses. She looked up and saw the wind carry a feather into a cluster of prickly pear. She wasn't collecting feathers, but this one had a red ribbon and leather tie on it. She picked it out of the thorny plant and stuck the end of the quill into the back of her hair where the long braid began. She thought the feather must make her look like one of the Indian girls from the tribe camped outside the fort.

Emily unsnapped the leash from Bruno's collar to let him

*"Bruno! Let go! Stop it!"*

have a final run as she walked back on the path near the cook wagon. Bruno ran on ahead, his ears flopping and long tail waving over his back.

Suddenly Emily heard excited barking. Then snarls and growls. When she rounded the wagon, there was Hawk. He was holding a flour barrel in his arms while trying to kick the dog loose from his pants leg. Bruno's teeth clamped firmly as he shook his head back and forth. The more Hawk kicked and pulled, the tighter the snarling dog held on. Hawk dropped the barrel and flour flew all over the ground, sending up a white cloud. He lost his balance and fell. Boy and dog rolled over and over on the flour-covered ground.

"Bruno! Let go! Stop it!" Emily rushed in and managed to snap the leash back on Bruno's collar. As she restrained the still growling dog, Hawk picked himself up and began to brush off the flour.

"What were you doing? Stealing our flour?" Emily didn't wait for an answer. "You know what the rules are for anyone caught stealing? You'll be whipped in front of everyone."

"I didn't mean to—"

"Your pa is really going to be mad when he finds out, and you'll get another whipping from him."

"Please don't tell the wagonmaster or Pa. Please. I promise I won't bother you any more." He continued to try to dust off the flour from his shirt, and then he set the flour barrel upright, replaced the lid, and put it carefully back in the wagon. "I didn't spill very much," he said.

Emily brushed flour from the dog's fur as best she could with her hand.

"Look at my trousers—where the dog tore them. It's the only pair I have. Now I *am* in trouble. What am I going to tell Pa about the rip?"

Emily tried to think what Mama would do.

"Doesn't your brother have an extra pair you can borrow?"

"Maybe."

"Go change and put the torn pair in the back of our freight wagon. I brought my sewing kit along, and I can mend them. And I won't tell on you this time." She shook her finger at him. "But I'm warning you, Hawk Hammond, don't mess around my cook wagon any more!"

Hawk tried to hold the gaping hole shut as he limped back to his wagon.

Bruno strained against his leash, and Emily was anxious to take him back to the fort. When she started through the big gate, her blue eyes met the steady gaze of a brown-eyed Indian girl who appeared to be about her age. The girl seemed to be interested in the long feather sticking in Emily's braid. Emily hesitated only a moment before she hurried on to Susan's room.

"I picked you some wildflowers," she said, handing Susan the bouquet.

"They smell good," Susan said. "That's a pretty feather in your hair."

"An Indian girl by the gate must have thought so too. She looked as if she wanted it."

"Let me see it," Susan said. She turned the feather over in her hand. "It's decorated in an unusual way. I believe this is a special Sioux feather that probably belongs to the girl you saw by the gate. When a Sioux girl becomes a woman, at about your age, it's a tribal custom to decorate her with a sacred eagle feather like this. From then on the tribe treats her as a woman, not as a girl."

"I'll bet she feels very special," Emily said.

Susan agreed. "Thank you for the flowers and for walking Bruno," she said. "Won't you sit down? Jane," she called out, "please bring us a drink of cool water from the well and put these lovely flowers in a vase."

Bruno lay down at Susan's feet. He wagged his long tail when his name was mentioned.

"Are you enjoying the trip with your father?" Susan asked.

"Yes, most of the time." Emily explained that Papa had reluctantly agreed to bring her along after Jed's accident.

"I'm sure both of you are doing a good job of helping your father," Susan said.

"I don't know. Sometimes Papa acts as if he's glad I came along, and other times he's mad about something I've done. I'm beginning to wonder if I should have stayed home." Emily reached for her mother's handkerchief.

Susan patted Emily's knee. "Think about it. Your father has a lot to do. He gets tired, very tired driving the wagon every day from sunup to sunset. That's why he's cranky with you. Things don't always go smoothly on the trail. An oxen can get sick, a

wagon wheel or tongue  can break, other traders need his help—
He has to deal with one thing after another."

Emily dabbed her eyes.

"My dear husband Samuel acts happy most of the time.
Other times  he won't tell me anything about his business, but
he goes off with the men and leaves me alone," she confided.
"Every day I try to be happy and cheerful when he is around and
not complain about anything, because I understand how hard
he's working to run his freighting business.   Would you like to
try my method with your father?"

"I'll try," Emily said, "but it's hard to be happy and cheerful
when you're sad on the inside."

"The day will come when your father will tell you how much
he appreciates all the things you're doing to help him," Susan
said. "Just wait and see."

"Thank you for  helping me." Emily tucked her handkerchief
back into her apron pocket and said she must be getting back.

The path Emily used to return to the  corral  was crowded
with people and  Conestoga wagons. The big freighters still held
their loads of merchandise  that would be traded in Santa Fe.
Some small farm wagons and pack mules carried beaver pelts
and bison skins the Arapahos and trappers had brought in to sell
at the Bent's Fort trading post.

As Emily walked  toward camp she looked for the Indian girl
who had admired the feather.  She wasn't anywhere to be seen.
Emily continued  walking toward their wagon circle in the meadow.  She stopped a moment to remove a small rock from her
shoe.  As she straightened up, the girl was standing beside her.
She pointed to the  feather in Emily's hair and then to herself.
Emily understood and handed it to her.  A broad smile spread
across the girl's face as she tucked the feather into her own hair.

Emily started to turn away. The native girl reached inside
her deerskin bag, brought out a small  beaded pouch, and handed it to Emily.

"Thank you," Emily said with a smile.

"You're welcome," the  girl signed, or at least that was what
Emily thought she meant.

Anyway, it seemed like a sign of friendship.

*Emily understood and handed the feather to her.*

CHAPTER 11

EMILY STIRRED THE HOT COALS UNDER THE COFFEE POT. The smell of coffee and baking cornbread drifted through the corral, drawing the interest of the men who began to gather around the cooking area.

"Breakfast's ready," Emily announced, motioning them to come. "Where's Papa?"

Shorty nodded his head in the direction of the main gate. Papa kicked loose dirt and dry grass ahead of him as he stormed into the camp site.

Emily handed him a tin cup of coffee and a plate of cornbread.

"We've been here five days and we still haven't seen hide nor hair of those soldiers from Fort Leavenworth who are supposed to escort us," he complained to the men as they sat around the fire. "If they don't get here soon, I'd be in favor of going on without them. I know we could make it—but Captain Summers says we have to obey military orders."

Emily looked at Papa, dipping his cornbread in his coffee. She wondered why he was so impatient. And then she understood why when she thought how often she felt the same way.

The men agreed with Matt, as they were getting restless too, and every man knew that a long delay would make the return trip just that much riskier as winter drew near.

After breakfast, Papa seemed to have resigned himself to waiting as long as necessary for the military escort. "Jed, after I finish my coffee let's go hunting," he suggested. "I hear the bison are nearby. Maybe we could bring Emily some fresh meat for a pot of stew."

Papa handed Jed a piece of rope. "Go get one of the gentlest mules to carry our load."

Emily watched the men take their guns out of the wagons and set off. She wished she could go hunting with them. As they had approached Bent's Fort, she remembered seeing bison herds in the distance. She had strained her eyes, but they were always too far away for her to see if there were any calves.

Later in the afternoon the sun began to cast long shadows. Emily started a big fire in the cooking pit, in anticipation of cooking bison stew. She filled two Dutch ovens with water, hung the heavy pots on tripods over the hot flames and covered one pot with a cast-iron lid. As she reached for the other cover with her "third-hand" tool, the heavy lid slid off and fell on her right foot.

"Ouch . . . that hurts!" She took off her shoe and felt her foot to see if any bones were broken. It ached when she rubbed the spot where the lid hit. She carefully stepped down on her foot to see if she could put her weight on it. A bruise was starting to appear. She tied a red bandana around her instep and sat on the ground by the water barrel.

What a day! Papa had been grumpy. He had tramped off in a huff to hunt bison without asking her to go. The next thing she knew, she had dropped the heavy lid on her foot. To make things worse, she had rubbed a blister on the heel of her left foot. She slumped over and held her forehead in her hands. Her feet hurt and she wished she were home. She had a good cry . . .

Soon Emily heard the hunters' voices. She dipped her hands into a bucket of water by the fire, washed her face and patted it dry with Mama's handkerchief. She was ready for the hunting party's return.

Jed, the first to arrive, led the heavily laden mule to the cook wagon and saw Emily limp over to help him unload the meat.

"What happened to you?"

"I dropped an iron lid on my foot. It hurts, but it isn't broken. I'm all right."

Others began to arrive. In all, it took four trips with the mule to pack in the meat from one animal. The mule seemed skittish, as if it didn't like the smell of blood.

"What a treat to have fresh meat again," Emily said as she and Jed unloaded the meat. "Where did you find the bison?"

"We found a herd a few miles west of the Arkansas River,"

he said.

"Oh . . . Did you get close enough to really see them?"

"Yes, they were grazing quietly—not bellowing or fighting with each other. Some rolled in the dust and shook their heads."

"Did you see any cows with new calves?"

"Yup, there were some young ones beside their mothers."

Emily frowned with disappointment. "The one thing I had most hoped to see on the trail was a baby bison."

"This is the best time of year to see newborn calves. If you really want to see one, ask Papa if he will take you out tomorrow."

Matt and the hunters returned with the rest of the meat. They shared it with others in the train. All were hungry for fresh meat so it was accepted gratefully.

"Papa, will you take me out to see the bison tomorrow? I do so want to get close enough to the herd to see a baby calf," Emily implored.

Papa noticed that she was limping. "Are you sure you feel up to walking?" he asked.

"Yes, it's nothing. I bruised my foot."

"All right. Be ready to leave after breakfast."


Emily awoke with the first light of day and cooked a special breakfast of fried liver and johnny cakes.

"That was a good meal. Now let's see if you're ready," Papa said. "Have your sunbonnet? And your shoes laced and tied around that sore foot? Looks to me like you're ready." He gave her arm a little squeeze.

Emily smiled at Papa's words of approval.

They started off at a lively pace toward the Arkansas River. She and Jed took long steps, trying to keep up with Papa. He carried a gun in case they might need it.

"We have to be prepared. We never know if the bison will be restless and dangerous or indifferent as they are most of the year. A bison's sense of smell and hearing are keener than their ability to see," he said. "So we'll stay downwind of the herd. Let's walk toward the river to see if we can find any there."

They walked quietly along a narrow animal trail.

"Emily," Jed said softly, "look at this tree. It must be one of their rubbing spots. The bark is stripped higher than Papa's head, and their matted hair is still hanging on the branches."

"Shhh. . ." Papa said. "They've been here. See this big dust hole. They roll in the dust to keep the insects from biting."

"Look down at the river!" Emily said. "The bison are swimming across."

Jed chuckled. "Aren't they funny the way they hold their noses and humps above the water? Their tails are waving in the air like flags!"

Emily wanted to get closer. "Look!" she said. "There's one white calf! All the rest are brown. Oh, a white one—" She could hardly take her eyes off the newborn calf as it stood up on wobbly legs and tried to follow its mother.

She gave Papa a quick hug for bringing her. "I was beginning to think I would never see a baby bison. Jed and I have seen an antelope, curlews and prairie chickens and, of course, thousands of jackrabbits. And now, finally, I get to see my first baby and it is white. Oh, thank you—"

Papa looked toward the trail, momentarily distracted. "Something's happening over there. See the dust in the sky? I wonder if the soldiers have finally arrived from Fort Leavenworth. If they have, that's probably why the bison scattered and swam across the river. We need to hurry back to the fort to see if they're here." He had changed back to his usual serious face.

*Day 51*

*Dear Diary,*

*The soldiers were noisy when they marched into the fort. We could hear the officer's loud orders down in our corral. The sight of so many military men frightened every Indian out of the courtyard.*

*I wasn't sure if Papa was going to be mad at me again & say I'd been careless because I dropped the cast-iron lid on my foot. He doesn't like to hear me complain, so I kept quiet about my sore foot.*

*Papa was so good to take me out to see the bison. He told me the Cheyennes believe the rare birth of a white bison is sacred & that white animals belong to the Sun God. If a white birth happens during a brave's lifetime it is supposed to bring him joy.*

*I will always remember seeing my first bison calf. It brought me joy.*

*E. J.*

## CHAPTER 12

"MEN, THE TROOPS HAVE FINALLY ARRIVED," Jake Summers, the wagon train captain, informed his four lieutenants. "Colonel Kearny and his soldiers will escort us into Santa Fe. The Mountain Route is the safest way to travel this time of the year—except for a treacherous stretch of trail along Raton Pass. The colonel has sent Captain Moore and some volunteers ahead to repair and clear big boulders from that fifteen-mile section of the mountain trail. All freighters will leave Bent's Fort within the next three days. Matt, your group will leave early in the morning."

Emily and Jed heard the orders. Papa turned to them. "Let's get our Conestoga and cook wagon ready," he said. "Pack the barrels and boxes tightly and tie down the canvas top securely. Traveling the Raton Pass will be a challenge for all of us. Finally! We are on our way!"

Emily hurried inside the fort to see Susan. With wagging tail Bruno greeted her as she entered Susan's room.

"How are you feeling today?"

"I'm a little bit better," Susan said. She was fully dressed, sitting in a rocking chair, holding a sampler she was embroidering. "We don't plan to leave tomorrow with the caravan because I'm not well enough to travel yet. But Samuel and I will catch up with you in a while in Santa Fe."

"I understand," Emily said, looking at the floor. "Before I leave could I ask you something that has been bothering me?"

"Of course, dear. What is it?"

Emily explained that she and her brother had seen the small black wagon and had tried to figure out who owned it.

"That Dearborn carriage belongs to Samuel and me. My maid Jane sleeps in it and we store our trunks in it," Susan said.

"But why was the driver so angry when we tried to look in?"

"You must not pay too much attention to Carlos," she said with a smile. "He is a little afraid of Jane, and he tries to keep things quiet so as not to disturb her during the day when she is sleeping. Her work begins in the evening when we stop to camp. Jane cooks our meals, keeps our clothes clean and mended, helps with the dog—"

"I'll miss you and I'll even miss Bruno," Emily said impulsively. "Let me give you a good-bye hug."

Through tears Emily admired the heart necklace  Susan wore with her white, lace trimmed summer dress. She thought Susan's face looked like one she had seen on a cameo brooch.

Early the next morning officers barked military commands to the soldiers. Papa helped organize their caravan to leave the fort. Outside the gate curious people gathered to watch the white-topped Conestogas begin to roll down the trail, one by one, on their way to Santa Fe.

The Mountain Route offered greater safety and water than the shorter Cimarron route. The wagon train followed the trail as it crossed the Arkansas River and continued up the Purgatoire to Trinidad, Colorado. At this junction the trail swung sharply south and the long line of freighters climbed the Raton Mountains to the entrance of the pass. They had finally reached that fifteen-mile pass that was considered the worst hazard on the route.

Matt stopped, looked down the rocky hill and scratched his chin. He shook his head as if he feared the worst but hoped for the best.

Prodding the lead yoke of oxen to start the heavy wagon rolling, he called out commands to control and calm the animals in this dangerous part of the pass. Earlier in the day he and the wagoners had blocked their wagon wheels with logs to keep them from rolling downhill too fast.

Matt cautiously guided the team down the steep trail. Emily walked on the left side of the wagon, Jed on the right. Slowly the oxen inched the freighter down the hill. Iron rims screeched as they rubbed against the jagged rocks.

Suddenly the sounds changed. Emily saw the wheels on her side slip down into a ditch. The wagon tilted sharply and teetered in a balance, ready to fall on its side at any moment.

"Help! The wagon's tipping!" she screamed. A swarm of men appeared out of nowhere. Some leaned their backs against the side of the wagon to steady it, while others lifted the wheels out of the ditch. The wagon swayed precariously before settling back into an upright position. The huge Conestoga continued to inch its way down the rocky pass, sliding and bumping, creaking and groaning all the way.

Jed and Emily walked together.

"I was scared when the wagon tilted toward me." Emily admitted, drawing in her breath with a shudder. "All I could think about was spilling all Papa's trade goods down the hill and maybe ruining the blue package—whatever is in it."

"Emily, don't worry. Everything's all right now," Jed said, giving her an awkward pat on the shoulder. "These things happen on the trail." His voice sounded older, almost like a man's.

"You're right. You're a good brother."

"Who, me?" He pulled his straw hat down over his ears and fluttered his eyelids.

"Yes, you!"

Jed ran around to check the other side of the wagon.

Emily sighed. She took a deep breath of the mountain air. The beauty and enormity of the snow-capped mountains were beyond anything she could have imagined. And the trail was an ever-changing landscape of prairie turning into desert, with interesting plants, cacti and sagebrush, and the strange tumble-weed that rolled into balls and traveled with the wind. None of the hardships they had experienced so far had made her truly regret persuading Papa to bring her along.

The next day the strain of moving the freighters was even worse than before. The men tied ropes to the wagons and physically moved them over the steepest rocky hills. It took most of the day to move them only 800 feet. Because of the rough roads and boulder fields the wagoners often had to stop and rescue overturned freighters or repair broken wagon tongues. In the distance, the constant rumble of wagon wheels could be heard as other wagons crossed the rocky terrain.

The men finally guided the last wagon through the pass and were ready to set up camp for the night. She heard them bragging and comparing stories about their narrow escapes. It had taken them five days to get down the pass, although it had seemed longer. They were on the prairie again, but this time they had mountains and pine trees all around. The men formed their wagon circle. Emily found her cook wagon and began to prepare a feast for the tired and hungry traders.

That evening, the men gathered around the campfire to make plans for entering Santa Fe the next day. As the sky turned from dusk to dark, a tall, thin shadow came between the flickering campfire and the cook wagon and moved toward Emily as she replaced her utensils and tied down the hood. It was Hawk.

He pulled a torn red bandana out of his pocket and wiped his brow. He wore the trousers she had mended for him. "Emily," he stammered, "I . . . I've got something to tell you."

She turned around to face him, her arms folded across her chest. "What is it?"

He spoke softly. "I put the snake in your coffee pot . . . "

"But why?"

He hesitated. He wrapped and re-wrapped the bandana around his left hand like a bandage. "I asked your father for a job, but then he turned me down because he decided to bring you along. I was mad because I didn't think a girl should be on our trip."

"I don't know why you thought that!" she said.

"I made a mistake . . . I've discovered that girls aren't so bad after all. I know you kept me from getting in trouble with Pa and the wagonmaster."

He swallowed hard. "Is there any way—I mean . . . Do you think . . . we could be friends?"

Emily was caught off guard. Hawk didn't seem so mischievous when he spoke this way. It took a lot of courage to own up to what he had done. "I'll think about it," she said. "You got me in trouble with Papa. He thought I was careless for letting a snake crawl in the coffee pot."

"Shall I go talk to him?"

"Oh, no! I'll deal with him myself," She was looking at the tall, ungainly boy in a different light. "I guess I'm not mad. Maybe we could be friends."

Hawk squared his shoulders. He looked down on her from his greater height. "Thanks, Emily, I feel better now. I gotta go back to the wagon." He started to walk away and then stopped. "Don't you live near Independence?"

"Yes."

"I live in Sibley—not far from you. When we get back home, maybe I could come over and see you . . . and Jed."

Emily smiled and looked away, but when she started to say something he already had disappeared.

# CHAPTER 13

THE LONG LINE OF COVERED WAGONS STRETCHED across a level prairie surrounded by towering mountains. Some peaks were dotted with sparse vegetation, others were massive hunks of jagged rock where nothing would grow. Above all, the big sky with fleecy, scudding clouds dwarfed the caravan, and the August sun beat down on the weary travelers without mercy.

Emily trudged along beside their wagon. It seemed they had been on the trail for a year, but actually it was barely three months. Her bruise had gone away and her blister had healed, but her feet were hot and tired—so tired of walking.

Jed carried a stick and wore his straw hat at a jaunty angle. His hair curled around his ears and down over his collar.

"Jed, I thought we'd be in Santa Fe long before now. Are we ever going to get there?"

"Sure. The rest of the trip will be easy compared to what we've been through. No more rivers. No more rocky passes. In the next couple of days, we'll be coming to some little villages where we'll see people—mostly Mexicans. Wait'll you see their funny houses made of mud and their fences made of sticks."

The first village they approached was Las Vegas. From a distance they saw sheep grazing on prairie grass and, when they drew close, sheep herders came up to the wagons and boldly tried to sell cheese, corn and green peppers.

Emily soon realized she was quite a curiosity to the dark-skinned people. They swarmed around her father's wagon and stared at her. One woman came close and seemed about to touch her long braid or her full-length calico dress. Emily, who had pushed her bonnet to her back, with the strings around her neck, now replaced her bonnet and tied the strings under her chin.

The friendly brown people watched as if she were putting on a show. But she also stared back at them. She had never seen women with their bare arms and necks exposed in public. She knew Mama wouldn't approve of their short skirts and low-cut blouses.

The next day the caravan passed through another settlement called San Miguel. It was different in that it had a church and a public square. But the wagon train stopped only briefly and soon rolled on down the trail in a cloud of dust.

A few minutes after quenching her thirst, Emily could again feel the grit in her teeth.

Jed was unusually cheerful. "Emily, this is the place I like best—Pecos Pueblo," he said, as they entered the next village. "Papa said we'd camp here tonight. It's our last night. Did you hear me? Our *last night*. Tomorrow we'll travel on into Santa Fe."

"I wish we were there now." Emily had never been so far from home. She kept trying to remember Mama's soft voice and her strong hands that could do many things. She had never known a time when Mama wasn't near, especially if she felt tired or sad.

"Emily, we're almost there, I promise."

The wagons pulled into their circles for the night and the travelers set up camp.

Papa sat on the ground and leaned against a wagon wheel. He was in a talkative mood as he relaxed and finished eating the prairie chicken stew from his tin plate. "The Pecos Indians once lived here," he said, "more than 2,000 of them. But the Comanches and diseases nearly wiped out the tribe. The last few Pecos survivors took their sacred fire and left to join the Jemez. All that's left here are the church and burying grounds. Why don't you children take a look around—see what you can see."

Jed and Emily ran off to find Hawk to help them explore the ruins of the Pecos Indian pueblo before nightfall. Emily had promised Papa she would wash the camp dishes and tidy up the cook wagon later by the light of the campfire and her lantern.

49

The next morning the campers began to stir before daylight. By sunup, the men had washed the grime of many miles of travel from their faces, wetted down and combed out their windblown hair, and each had dressed in his best suit of clothes. Some of the men even took time to tie new leather "crackers" to the ends of their whips. When they finally reached Santa Fe, the drivers would use their whips to show off and try to outdo each other when driving through the streets.

The miles rolled away, and Emily's excitement mounted. She strained her eyes for that first glimpse of Santa Fe. In her imagination it ranked right up there next to heaven, with streets paved of gold.

When they had only a few miles left to go, the caravan emerged onto an open plain. The air was clear and they could see for miles around. Groves of trees bordered corn and wheat fields.

The drivers urged their oxen forward and the slow-moving wheels began to turn faster, stirring up clouds of the ever-present dust.

"Where are we now?" Emily shouted to Jed.

"Almost there."

"But I see cornfields . . . we have those at home . . ."

"Look beyond the cornfields and you'll see Santa Fe."

"Where—? That's Santa Fe?" She shaded her eyes. "Is that all there is to Santa Fe? All I can see are adobe houses. From here it looks like a big brickyard with bricks scattered all around." She tried to swallow her disappointment. "Where are the buildings and houses like we have?"

"Silly girl, you are not in Independence now! You'll like the natives," he reassured her. "They are nice and friendly."

The sleepy town of Santa Fe began to come to life when the white-topped wagons rolled down the narrow streets and into the plaza at the center of town. Merchants and residents from all around were glad to see the wagon trains arrive with their special cargo of dry goods, hardware and other necessities.

"Whoa," Matt yelled to his lead oxen. The natives backed away from the sweating teams until they came to a full stop in the plaza. They called out words of welcome and gathered around the wagon. Native boys tried to lift a corner of the canvas hood on Matt's wagon to get a peek at his cargo.

Emily felt all eyes on her. Papa had said no women or girls traveled with the caravans, so she knew she stood out from her fellow travelers. Now she wished she had brought her Sunday dress along. She looked down at the clean, but faded homespun dress she had put on that morning, and she was embarrassed because the hem was frayed. She had grown taller since Mama made the dress, and her skirt didn't cover her ankles. By this time she was almost getting used to being stared at. What would Mama do in this situation? Emily smiled and tried to enjoy the attention from the curious people.

Matt Johnson was all business. "Emily and Jed, come with me. The first thing we need to do is sell our merchandise to one of the stores. Let's try a merchant I've dealt with before. I know someone who has always given me a fair price."

Dr. Henry Connelly, the first store owner Matt asked, agreed to buy the entire load of trade goods. He was especially interested in the large amount of white fabric they had brought—a scarce commodity the local women needed. They negotiated terms for the transaction and shook hands.

In due time the big freighter was unloaded—except for the blue package which Papa now took charge of—and it was pulled, empty and rattling, back to the camp site. Papa and Jed walked the animals to the pasture near the adobe houses at the edge of town where they could feed and rest. Guards were left to watch them.

Emily and Jed looked around them at the strange sights and sounds in the plaza market. Everywhere open air booths were packed with food, red and blue corn in baskets, melons piled high on dirt floors, and huge jars filled to the brim with Mexican beans. Luscious peaches, grapes and apples. Shiny red and green dried peppers hung in crowded bunches by every door.

Burros loaded with bundles of pinon firewood for sale were led around, mingling the fragrance of the pinon tree with the aroma of cooking food and other people and animal smells.

Papa had gone back to the wagon to rest. He had told Emily and Jed they could explore the town, but they must be sure to stay together. They joined a noisy crowd gathered in the plaza to celebrate the arrival of the caravan. They watched the natives dance to the music of a fiddle, guitar and drum. The women dancers snapped their fingers, stomped their feet and twirled their full, flared skirts to the beat of the lively music.

Emily leaned closer to her brother's ear and cupped a hand around her mouth. "I see now why the men cleaned up and slicked their hair back and wore their best clothes." She giggled. "They look funny trying to dance with the women in their clumsy shoes."

Jed smiled. He had never seen Shorty kick so high.

"The Mexican men and women wear such bright colored clothes. I wish I could have a red dress. I feel sort of like a brown sparrow in a flock of tropical birds." (She had seen their colorful plumage in a book at school.)

Jed was not interested in talking about clothes or birds. "Let's go back to the wagon and get something to eat," he said.

The next day, when the animals were rested, repairs made, and the other traders had sold their goods, Papa called to Emily and Jed.

"We have one more important job to do before we leave. We have to deliver the blue package for Mr. Aull. Emily, you took such good care of it on the trip, why don't you open the envelope and we'll see what our instructions are."

Emily's fingers trembled as she carefully opened the seal on the worn envelope. She took out the note and read aloud:

> *Please deliver this package to the priest*
> *at the Church of Saint Francis.*
> *Thank you for taking care of this imported*
> *silk altar cloth from China.*
> > *Sincerely,*
> > *Father Keegan*
> > *Saint Louis, Missouri*

Half an hour later the three of them walked up to the Church of St. Francis, an adobe building with two bell towers, and entered through a heavy wooden door. The air was hushed and cool and the church was slightly dark.

Inside they were greeted by a priest wearing a black robe. He seemed surprised when Emily handed him the package.

"Please sit down while I see what this is." He tore away the blue paper and read the note. "How nice of Father Keegan to send an altar cloth!" He held up the snowy white cloth with silver threads. "This will look elegant under the candles and Bible."

Emily thought she had never seen such a beautiful piece of fabric. The silver threads glistened when they caught the light from the open doorway. Her eye fell on a small madonna carved from wood. How different the adobe church was from the churches back home.

"Father Keegan was here last year," the priest explained, "and he must have seen our threadbare altar cloth. Thank you so much for bringing this all the way from Independence."

Papa and the priest made small talk about the trip and the weather, when suddenly their conversation was drowned by the clamor of bells. The ringing bells bombarded the air with sounds—loud, metalic tones that lingered, pleasant yet discordant. And on and on they rang.

Jed put his hands over his ears. Emily stood transfixed, hugging her arms across her chest where she could feel the reverberations of the bells. The chimes spilled all over each other. She thought it was a glorious sound!

The priest closed the door. "You are just in time to join us for the Angelus—our time of prayer," he said. "Please stay and hear the Franciscans chanting their ancient prayer. And perhaps you would like to give thanks for your safe trip."

When the service was over, the priest shook hands all around. "God be with you as you return to your home," he said.

They stepped out into the street, blinking their eyes to adjust to the bright sunlight.

Papa turned to Emily and Jed. "I'm proud of both of you for all the help you gave me on this trip. I don't have two children, I have two grown-ups. Emily, you were the little girl I called 'Sunshine' when we started out, but now you've grown into a young woman. I'm glad you came on this trip with me."

Emily gave her father a big hug. "You made my dream come true, Papa. Thank you for bringing me."

Papa smiled. "Jed, I couldn't have hired a man to do as good a job as you have done this year."

Jed, who had been carrying his straw hat, plopped it on his

head and pulled it down low to shade his eyes. But that did not cover the big grin that spread across his face.

The traders had rested their tired bodies and filled their stomachs with Mexican food, and they had reloaded their wagons with furs, tin, and other goods to take back to Missouri. Now it was time, though still in the middle of summer, to start the long trip back east in order to reach home before the winter storms set in.

The morning dawned bright and clear. Drivers hitched up their oxen early, and their wagons filled the streets of Santa Fe, awaiting the signal to line up.

Matt and Jed greased the wagon wheels with tar and made a last minute check of the cargo.

"All's set," "All's set," echoed the calls from each trader, as the cracking of bull whips rang out.

At that moment Emily saw the Magoffin wagons drive into the plaza. Their stay in Bent's Fort had delayed their arrival by several days.

"Oh, Papa, can you wait until I see Susan?" she pleaded. "Her wagon has just now driven up. Please give me a few minutes."

Papa wore his stern face, and seemed about to say "no." He glanced around at the other wagons. "Make it short. We're about ready to leave."

Emily gathered up her skirts and ran to her friend. "I'm glad to see you!"

"Emily, I'm glad to see you, too," Susan said with a smile, holding out both her hands. Her eyes had regained their sparkle and she had a faint glow of color in her cheeks.

Bruno barked and jumped up on Emily, wagging his tail wildly.

"I came to say good-bye because we're ready to go back to Missouri," Emily said. "Will you ever come to Independence—?"

"Emily Johnson, come on!" Papa called.

Emily could hardly speak because of the lump in her throat. She reached down and patted Bruno's head.

"I want to give you something to remember me by," Susan said. She unhooked the gold heart necklace from around her neck and spread it over her hand. "I want you to have this . . .

my mother gave it to me when I was just your age. I hope it will always remind you of this trip and of our friendship."

Emily drew in her breath. She stared at the golden heart on the delicate chain—her very first piece of jewelry.

"Dear, will you lift your braid and let me fasten it? I surely will be back in Independence some day. We will meet again."

"Oh! It's so—" Emily remembered her manners. "Thank you, Susan." She threw her arms around the pretty lady and gave her a tight hug. "I'll never forget you," she whispered in Susan's ear.

Emily fished in her pocket and brought out her favorite smooth, speckled stone and handed it to Susan. They said their good-byes and she reached once more in her pocket for Mama's handkerchief.

*Day 76*

*Dear Diary,*

*Dreams do come true. We made it to Santa Fe & now we're one day out, on our way home.*

*I'm happy & I'm sad.*

*Happy we made the trip safely & Papa sold the trade goods & bought more. Happy I met Susan. I'll treasure the beautiful necklace.*

*I loved seeing all the different flowers & animals along the way. But I'm glad to be going home to Mama & Grandma & Grandpa.*

*Sad because it might be a long time before I see Susan again.*

*I will always remember this trip. When I started out I felt like a little girl, & now I am almost grown.*

*Going to Santa Fe has taught me something. Girls & women can do whatever they set their minds & hearts to do.*

*E. J.*

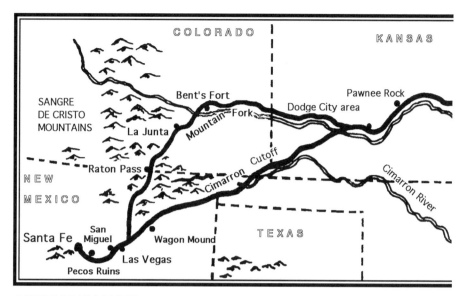

## AUTHOR'S NOTE:

The Santa Fe Trail played an important role in the expansion of the American frontier. The trail was the West's major trade artery in the nineteenth century. It linked Franklin, Missouri, and later Independence, Missouri—both located on the Missouri River—with Santa Fe and Chihuahua, Mexico.

William Becknell is credited with being the first white man to travel this commercial trail to Santa Fe. In the years before Becknell made his first trip, several groups had ventured west in hopes of opening up a trade route. Spain claimed Santa Fe and American traders were not welcome in what later became the capital of New Mexico.

In 1821, Mexico won its independence from Spain. That same year, Missouri became a state. Becknell packed mules with goods to trade and made the long trek to sell his merchandise. He made a handsome profit. The following year instead of taking pack mules or horses, he used wagons to haul cargo from Missouri to Santa Fe.

By that time attitudes had changed and Santa Fe officials welcomed the newly legalized commerce and encouraged traders to bring caravans carrying merchandise to their settlement. Prairie merchants from the East found that their trade flourished and profits soared.

In 1830, the trail expanded into two main routes with other variations. Both ran westward across Kansas through Council Grove to the Dodge City area. The Mountain Fork followed the Arkansas River west to a point near La Junta, Colorado, then turned south through Raton Pass. The Cimarron Cutoff also crossed the Arkansas River west of the Dodge City area and swung south around the Sangre de Cristo Mountains and into Santa Fe.

In 1846, rumors of war with Mexico spread among the traders bound for Santa Fe. In spite of the threat, some chose to proceed at their own risk. A bloodless conquest ended the Mexican War in 1848. The wagon trains continued to deliver their cargo. New Mexico was added to the United States.

Commerce boomed over the trail until the Civil War began in 1861; then all commercial trade ceased. After the war ended in 1865, trading revived immediately and continued to thrive until the use of the trail for transporting goods was eclipsed by the completion of the Atchison, Topeka and Santa Fe Railroad in 1880. Slow moving freight wagons could not compete with the railroad's efficient transportation that provided year-round delivery.

# BIBLIOGRAPHY

Brown, William E. *The Santa Fe Trail.* Tucson, Arizona: The
    Patrice Press, 1988.

Gregg, Josiah. *The Commerce of the Prairies.* Lincoln, Nebraska:
    University of Nebraska Press, 1967.

Lavender, David. *Bent's Fort.* Garden City, New York: Dolphin
    Books, Doubleday and Company, 1954.

Magoffin, Susan Shelby. *Down the Santa Fe Trail and into
    Mexico.* Lincoln,Nebraska: University of Nebraska Press,
    1962.

Maxwell, James A., ed. *America's Fascinating Indian Heritage.*
    Pleasantville, New York: Reader's Digest Assn., 1978.

Russell, Marian. *Land of Enchantment.* Albuquerque, New
    Mexico: University of New Mexico Press, 1981.

Simmons, Marc. *On the Santa Fe Trail.* Lawrence, Kansas:
    University Press of Kansas, 1986.

Walker, Henry Pickering. *The Wagonmasters.* Norman,
    Oklahoma: University of Oklahoma Press, 1966.

Webb, David. *Adventures with the Santa Fe Trail.* Dodge City,
    Kansas: Kansas Heritage Center, 1989.

## ABOUT THE AUTHOR

A Midwesterner all her life, Evelyn Bartlow was born in
Drexel, Missouri, and has lived for many years in Kansas City,
Missouri. Her interest in history led her to become a docent at
the 1858 John Wornall House Museum, where she gives tours
to visitors of all ages. Mrs. Bartlow also serves as an outdoor
trainer in Mid-Continent Council of Girl Scouts' adult education
program, and she is an avid environmentalist. Dating back to
her studies in elementary education  at the University of
Missouri-Kansas City, her interest in children and education
has continued. She is married to Charles Bartlow and they
have two grown children.